An Interactive Adventure

WARRIOR
A LEGEND BEGINS!

Book 1: The Blood Crown Quest

By Adam C. Mitchell
and
Lukas Latham {Aged 10}

©Copyright 2021

WARRIOR - A LEGEND BEGINS!
BOOK I: THE BLOOD CROWN QUEST
ISBN: 9798709212480

© 2021 Originally self-published in Shrewsbury, Shropshire, UK, - Print on Demand

© Copyright AcM Gamebooks 2021

The right of Adam C Mitchell to be identified as the author of this book, has been asserted by them in accordance with the © Copyright, Designs and Patents Act 1988.

Conditions of Sale:
This book is sold subject to the condition that it shall not, by way of trade or otherwise, be lent, re-sold, hired out, or otherwise circulated, or stored in any form of binding or cover, other than that in which it is published, and without a similar condition, including this condition, being imposed on the subsequent purchaser.

This book is sold subject to the Standard Conditions of Sale of Net Books and may not be sold anywhere, below the Net price fixed by the author of this book.
***
References to Rise of the Ancients and Shadow Thief: Jailbreak, are used with permission from their respective authors.
***

Both of the Authors would like to thank
Louise, Troy, Derek, Steve, Graham
and the rest of the Gamebook Authors Guild.

"This book is dedicated to my Mum!"
- love, Lukas

INTRODUCTION

The year is 2020, and well, the world has gone down the drain. The Mitchell clan, like most of the UK, were in lockdown due to the Covid-19 Pandemic. And so, madness was slowly building — madness and panic — especially when the UK Government closed the schools. To kill the boredom, and to avoid me wanting to wring the neck of my eldest, Lukas (aged 10), I introduced him to a certain gamebook series and role-playing game of which I cannot name for copyright reasons. Well, it sparked his imagination, and he wrote the book that you are about to read. All I did was tidy it up and tweak it here and there, but the general feel and tone of the book was devised by him. So sit back and enjoy the tale that is about to unfold.... (He has a few more books planned, so this may turn into a small series.... Time will tell!)

HOW IT ALL BEGINS

In the tapestry-hung antechamber of the Wizards' Guild, a warm fire burns in the iron grate, and a robed, bearded figure rises to greet you. His bearing is fierce, but his expression is not unfriendly.

"Welcome, Warrior! I, Arudus, the Grand Wizard of this Guild, offer you a chance to become a true hero of this realm, for times are dire and heroes are in short supply. If you would tread the path of a true hero, you must first walk the path of danger through the dungeons of this Guild."

If you accept the challenge set to you by the Grand Wizard, arm yourself with a pencil and paper with which to record the items and spells you may collect. You will also need a six-sided die, as chance will play a significant part in what lies ahead. Once you have read the rules that follow, you will be ready to start.

THE RULES OF WARRIOR

Rule 1:
Your Health in this gamebook series has three possible grades: GREEN, AMBER and RED. You begin the adventure on GREEN, indicating that you are un-wounded and fresh for the challenge.

At intervals during the adventure, you will be informed whether you have lost or gained a Health Grade. For instance, if you are on AMBER and you are told to lose a Grade, your Health would change to RED. If you are already on RED, any further loss of health will kill you!

Rule 2:
You can consume any item of food or drink at any time when at an entry marked with an asterisk {*}. Each item of food or drink will increase your Health by one Grade.

Rule 3:
You can carry up to five objects at one time. If you find an item that you would like to take, but already have five items, you must discard one first.

Rule 4:
You will sometimes be given spells to use during the course of the adventure, but you cannot possess more than three spells at any time. Most spells are useful in several situations, but you must choose the right moment to use them, as they can only be used once.

YOUR ADVENTURE BEGINS NOW...
GOOD LUCK, WARRIOR!

1

You wrap your fingers around the hilt of your sword and secure your shield to your arm. As you are about to enter the dungeon below the Guild, Arudus presents you with a choice — you can either learn a new spell or take a loaf of bread to eat later on.

- You take a loaf of bread. Make sure to write it down, and then turn to **20**
- You decide to learn a spell - turn to **152**

2

"A wise choice!" you hear the voice of the wizard in your head. "Opening that chest would have been nasty indeed. Sometimes caution is required with such things!"

Next to the chest is a small archway. Stepping through, you head down another flight of stairs to a lower level of the dungeon.

- Now, Warrior, turn to **145**

3

"A strong choice!" admits the wizard. "You have gained the HAMMER spell. Once cast, it can be used to hit or destroy something incredibly hard, but the recoil can knock you off of your feet, so be warned...."

(Make sure you have the spell in mind, by writing it down). You leave the arena.

- Now, Warrior, turn to **145**

4

You descend the stairs into another dark passage. You walk down the long corridor until your way is blocked by a door. You reach for the door's handle, but your hand is hit by a stabbing pain, and pulling it back, notice bite marks. You peer down at the handle and observe that it is alive — most likely due to an enchantment.

Then, you hear it speak. "Answer my riddle and I will give you passage. My riddle is this:

I share a common fate with the sea, spinning the months around in alternate cycles. When the glory of my light-flowing form wanes, so too, the sea loses its swollen flood tides."

If your answer is:

- The Moon, turn to **43**
- The Sun, turn to **142**
- The Calendar, turn to **54**
- The River, turn to **40**

5

With the last ounce of your energy and strength, you fire directly at the eye. The arrow flashes across the chamber, but never reaches its target. You have died.

(For you, Warrior, the challenge has ended! For you, it's Game Over, I'm afraid! Better luck next time).

6

"Ah," says Arudus. "This spell creates a force field which can protect you against 'virtually' any attack, but only for a short time."

(Make sure that you have the spell in mind, by writing it down). Get ready to begin your quest!

- Now, Warrior, turn to **20**

7

As you rematerialize on the other side of the portal, you hear the Wizard's voice fill the room. "DANGER! This Chamber is mined and is on a very short fuse. Now would be a good time to move, don't you think?"

You scan the room as quickly as you can and spot exits to the left and right of you. Which one will you choose?

Will you:

- Go left - turn to **133**
- Go right - turn to **102**

8

You stagger back, certain that the second stroke of this sword-wielding woman of the cloth will send you to meet your divine maker. But then, she gazes at your face more closely and puts up her sword.

"In this darkness, I mistook you for someone else," she states solemnly. "My apologies!"

You feel like letting rip and shouting at her, but discerning the steely look in her eyes, you decide against it.

"You will call me matron!" she insists. "Now, say this, May I be excused, matron?"

Already injured and with more than enough of your blood staining her blade, you do as your told. You never considered nuns to be scary until today.

As you leave, the nun begins to feel repentance for her prior actions and offers you the ESCAPE spell. (To use it, make sure that you have the spell in mind, by writing it down).

She and her sword go back to praying.

You see two archways leading back out into the dungeon.

- You take the eastern archway - turn to **58**
- You take the western archway - turn to **77**

9 - 10

9

You notice two levers that control the right and middle doors. A single rope between them seems to hold a counterweight that drops the gates. Maybe hitting the rope will help.

Unstrapping the longbow from your shoulder, you nock an arrow to the bowstring and take careful aim. You let the arrow fly, hitting the rope with heroic ease. The ancient mechanism grinds and the iron obstacles open.

(You may keep the longbow, as you have plenty of arrows left).

- You take the left exit - turn to **18**
- You take the middle exit - turn to **38**
- You take the right exit - turn to **17**

10

He peers down at you with his one eye and emits a strange cackle. "I climbed up here to get my two pet ravens, but they flew off and now I'm caught. Give an old man a hand, will you?"

- If you leave him up there, turn to **126**
- If you decide to help, turn to **83**

11

{*} The passage emerges into a torture chamber, where several burning braziers give off an intense, smoky heat. You see a stone archway opposite you, and on the floor near to it lies a large, misshapen sack. To your left is a serving girl, who sits rather morosely on the flagstones. It is clear that she has been badly abused and beaten. She is gagged and bound to the wall by a chain wrapped around her weak wrists. To the right, is a large blackboard bearing what looks like some foreign tongue or incantation upon it. Either way, you are unable to read it.

What will you do?

- Remove the girls gag - turn to **101**
- Break her chain (if you have the chisel) - turn to **113**
- Use the chalk on the blackboard - turn to **32**
- Decide to simply leave, and not get involved - turn to **69**

12

As you cast the KNIGHT spell, a strong astral knight appears. He has a stout shield strapped to his arm and a mean longsword in his hand. You command the astral knight to attack. Within moments, your enemy is no more. You thank the knight, who promptly disappears with a bow. (You have used this spell and will not be able to cast it again).

As you search for an exit, you discover a small sprig of green plant growing from a crack in the rock by a small door.

(You touch the plant and your Health Grade resets and is back on GREEN).

- Turn to **149**

13

"The pool of Wisdom..." sniggers the old man, "a good choice."

Suddenly, you flinch back. To you disgust, there seems to be an eye floating under the water.

- If you go ahead and fill the bottle anyway, turn to **74**
- If you prefer to try another pool, turn to **83**

14

Boulderax bellows a hollow laugh. "WRONG! Now I shall devour you!"

His massive stone jaws crunch down, but suddenly, an astral hand appears and you are hurled backwards by it, so that instead of being crushed to death, you are only badly hurt. (Lose ONE Health Grade).

If you survive this, you hear Arudus and the Rock Monster arguing. Using this as a distraction, you make a break for it.

- Turn to **36**

15

As you reach the threshold, a giant, magical hand seizes you and hurls you through the darkness. The force of the throw sends your sword flying from its scabbard, and it is lost in the black void. In the dungeons below the guild, the various chambers and rooms are not connected in the normal, physical sense, so merely walking from one to another is not always possible. Sometimes you will be transported by magic, and although disconcerting at first, you will get used to it.

You land in a heap, finding yourself confronted by a horrific, Giant Scorpion. It rushes towards you, its lethal stinger raised. There is only one exit from this chamber — an open portal roughly ten metres away.

What will you do?

- Make a frantic dash for the exit portal - turn to **122**
- Try to dodge the Giant Scorpion - turn to **29**

16

The shimmering portal takes you to a small corridor. You follow it a short way only to reach a small dusty library. All of the books are chained to the shelves, so you cannot take them down. It probably does not matter, as they are most likely written in the ancient tongue, which you cannot read.

An old woman comes out from behind one of the book stacks carrying a rather hefty book. "Help me with this, will you?"

It is Asphodel, the Great Fairy and Queen of the Fae, in human form.

- If you have the beechwood wand, turn to **141**
- If not, turn to **55**

17

You step through the right arch and a portal takes you into a small antechamber. The chamber is bathed in a strange, green glow, which issues forth from a menacing eye in the centre of the wall ahead of you.

"DANGER!" booms Arudus. "That is the eye of the Dark Lord... Be careful, Warrior. If he is permitted to feed and to regain his strength, the Dark One will escape the maze that I imprisoned him in and all will be lost."

Even as you gaze upon it, you feel your Health Grades seeping away. (Drop your Health Grade down to RED).

"The eye will never stop feeding... You MUST act swiftly!" Arudus adds.

(If you have the IRONWILL spell, cast it now to return your Health Grade to GREEN).

- Use the longbow and fire an arrow at it - turn to **5**
- Use the shield - turn to **160**

18
You step through the left-hand exit and into a portal, only to be trapped instantly within the thick, sticky net of a huge web. It is then that you see it — a Giant Spider rattling towards you. The sticky web renders any attempt at reaching for your longbow futile. You can wave your shield at it, but all that does is annoy it further. You have no chance. You are as good as dead, and for you, Warrior, the challenge has ended! It's Game Over, I'm afraid! Better luck next time.

19
You manage to pick the lock with mere seconds to spare. Opening the door quickly, you step through and slam it shut behind you. The bomb explodes, rocking the door. In the blast, the bolts of the door are blown out and one pierces your shoulder, impaling you. (Lose ONE Health Grade). You do your best, painfully, to free yourself, and then apply a piece of your tunic as a bandage. Once the bleeding has stopped, you decide to push on.

- Now, Warrior, turn to **145**

20

You step through the dungeon door and cautiously take a few steps. Once you have crossed the door's threshold, it closes and vanishes — there is no going back now. You find yourself in a chamber with a small brazier lighting up two seemingly innocent doors — one on the left and one on the right.

Which door do you take?

- You choose the door on the left - turn to **15**
- You choose the door on the right - turn to **25**

21

Beyond the arch, you step into a maze of interconnecting passages. Cautiously, you edge your way down the narrow stone corridors, positive that some great treasure must await you in the centre of the maze.

At last, you reach a point where the corridors all meet, and there before your eyes is a marble fountain whose water sparkles like diamonds and the rarest of jewels. You drink without a second thought and the enchanted waters restore you. (Your Health Grade is now back at GREEN).

While you are splashing the blessed water onto your face, you notice an object glittering at the bottom of the fountain. You fish it out — it is a golden key! You have a feeling that it will come in handy later.

Turning to retrace your steps, your heart sinks. Which way did you come? You look from passage to passage, but they all appear identical.

If you have one of the following, perhaps it will help you find a way out...

- A compass - turn to **65**
- A piece of parchment - turn to **148**
- A rat carving - turn to **51**
- Or, none of the above - turn to **42**

22

Boulderax bellows a hollow laugh. "WRONG! Now I shall devour you!"

His massive stone jaws crunch down, but an astral hand suddenly appears and you are hurled backwards by it, so that instead of being crushed to death, you are only badly hurt. As you land, you hear something break. (Lose TWO Health Grades).

If you survive this, you hear Arudus and the Rock Monster arguing and use this distraction to make a break for it.

- Turn to **36**

23

You raise the horn to your lips and blow a loud blast. Rather than the wall coming down around you, which you expected to happen, a large astral hand grabs you and hurls you through the brick wall. (Lose TWO Health Grades).

Beyond the rubble is a staircase to a deeper part of the dungeon.

- If you survive, turn to **4**

24

You make for the right-hand door and come face-to-face with a Cerberus that is guarding it. The huge door is decorated with blood and rather nasty claw marks. There is no way that you would survive a fight with such a beast. Yes, you have a longbow, but you suspect that your arrows would simply annoy it. Your only hope is a spell. (If you do not have any spells, then it's Game Over, I'm afraid).

- If you have the SLEEP spell, turn to **161**
- If you have the STEALTH spell, turn to **162**
- If you have the AGILITY spell, turn to **163**

25

As you reach the threshold, a giant magical hand seizes you and hurls you through the darkness. The force sends your sword flying from its scabbard only to be lost in the blackness of the void. In the dungeons below the guild, the various chambers and rooms are not connected in the normal, physical sense, and merely walking from one to another is not always possible. Sometimes you will be transported by magic, and although disconcerting at first, you will get used to it.

You land in a heap, and picking yourself up, find yourself in a broad empty chamber with two wooden doors as exits.

What will you do?

- You decide to take the door on the right, turn to **37**
- You decide to take the door on the left, turn to **105**

26

The robed figure cracks his knuckles and you see two, ruby-red eyes glowing beneath the hood of his black robe.

"I can hear a tongue wagging, but surely no brains are in that head of yours. That is the wrong answer!"

He clicks his fingers and a huge granite spire bursts from beneath you, impaling you from naval to nose.

(You are dead, and for you, Warrior, the challenge has ended! For you, it's Game Over, I'm afraid! Better luck next time).

27

You release yourself from the winch and cautiously push on deeper into the dungeons below the Wizards' Guild. You go on for a short distance and reach a vestibule with an alcove in the side wall to the right. It appears that a halfling in a tattered cloak has set up a stall of sorts here. Seeing you, he points to the wares laid out in front of him.

"What's this?" you ask.

The halfling waves his hand with a flourish. "It's a heroic pit-stop of sorts... Me and that cranky, old Arudus have... an... arrangement of sorts. You see, I say if a warrior or whatever, like yourself, gets this far, then they deserve a rest. He didn't like it at first... but a halfling is good at nagging, so he gave in eventually, and here I am. Oh, the name's Derek Underhill, by the way."

You look over the objects on display and at their rather hefty price tags, and see the following: winged sandals, a chisel, a piece of chalk, a crucifix, and a beechwood wand.

"Any of these items might be useful, but because the old wizard is a bit cooky, he has cursed a few. So be careful, there are a few red herrings chucked in there as well!" Derek claims with a flourished wave, and then looks at you expectantly.

"I'm afraid the price tags on all of these items are a little too high for my tastes," you grumble.

27 Continued - 29

Derek looks furtively at you, and then leans in and whispers. "Well, as long as you don't tell the big crank, I'll let you have them on credit. Take any two that you want."

- Select the two items that you want and make a note of them. Thanking Derek for his help, you continue along the corridor - turn to **82**

28
{*} The portal takes you into an oak-panelled passage, which soon leads you to a junction. A flicker of light comes from one of the two branches ahead of you, so you decide to go that way.

- Now, Warrior, turn to **75**

29
Why be cautious with a Giant Scorpion? Your only hope was to make a dash for the exit portal, but now it is too late — you are dead!

(For you, Warrior, the challenge has ended! For you, it's Game Over, I'm afraid! Better luck next time).

30

You agree, (and your Health Grade drops to RED). As you open it, a Shadow Boggart explodes out with a whoosh of air, cursing you and your belongings. (Your inventory is now cursed! Your inventory cap has decreased from 5 items to just 2, and all of your possessions and spells have been eliminated! Now collecting items and spells again is possible, but removing the Boggart's curse is a little bit trickier).

Next to the chest is a small archway. Stepping through it, you head down another flight of stairs to a lower level of the dungeon.

- Now, Warrior, turn to **145**

31

The vile Boggart instantly awakens and springs up, spitting curses. (Roll a six-sided die. If you roll a 5 or a 6, the Boggart has paralysed you. If that is the case, you are as good as dead, and for you, Warrior, the challenge has ended! For you, it's Game Over, I'm afraid! Better luck next time).

- If you score a 1 or a 2, you gave the Boggart such a painful kick (no doubt, to the groin), that it runs off - turn to **146**

- If you score a 3 or a 4, it rakes you with its talons, causing the loss of ONE Health Grade, but you still manage to run away - turn to **69**

32 - 33

32

The chalk on the old worn-out blackboard makes a horrid screeching noise, causing the serving girl to squirm. What a horrid person you are, to put an innocent girl through that kind of torture. Still, you are about to get what is coming to you, for the 'sack' in the corner suddenly springs to its feet and you see it now, in its horrific, true form — a vile Boggart!

"You're next!" it moans, as it clubs you over the head and chains you up beside the serving girl.

(You are as good as dead, and for you, Warrior, the challenge has ended! For you, it's Game Over, I'm afraid! Better luck next time).

33

The old man claps his hands. "The pool of life!" he cries. "Excellent choice!"

(The filled bottle counts as ONE item. You can drink it at any entry marked with an asterisk {*} and it will immediately restore your Health Grade to GREEN).

Suddenly, a rainbow appears over the old man, and he vanishes.

- Now, Warrior, turn to **126**

34 - 36

34

On top of the chest is a name plate, with a series of letters engraved upon it.

O S L E O W E P T N O M E T O Y A D G R O E U O E

- Yes - turn to **30**, or No - turn to **2**

35

"A clever choice!" muses the wizard. "You have gained the SLEEP spell. Once cast, this will put any creature or person into an almost coma-like sleep for about 10 minutes."

(Make sure you have the spell in mind, by writing it down). You leave the arena.

- Now, Warrior, turn to **145**

36

As you step through, you are flung by unseen forces into the darkness, only to stop when you hit a masonry column. (Lose ONE Health Grade) Grasping your ribs, which you believe might be broken, it is then that you notice out of the corner of your eye burning fuses that have almost reached their explosive targets. This chamber room is mined, and there is no time to lose!

There are exits to the left and right of you. Which will you choose?

- Left - turn to **63**, or right - turn to **112**

37

You walk along a passage that eventually opens up into a long room. There is a table here covered with mice gnawing at some stale crusts of bread. As you step forward, there is a rustling from behind the once grand tapestries, and several ugly Goblins scuttle out into the room from concealed passages. The way that they move, reminds you of giant spiders. Each wears a grin that displays their sharp, yellow teeth, and they are all armed with rusting swords and daggers.

What will you do?

- If you decide to fight them, turn to **89**
- If you try to dash past them, turn to **85**
- If you choose to retreat, turn to **68**

38

You find yourself in a round room with two doors — one to the left and one to the right. A huge, sand timer is ticking down and it appears that its time is almost up. You do not want to know what will happen when it runs out.

What will you do?

- Take the left door - turn to **24**
- Take the right door - turn to **57**

39

As you step through the portal, you arrive in a narrow stone corridor that seems to go on for a few metres. A trio of small braziers light the walls — just enough for you to observe row upon row of chiselled-out holes in the wall. Eyeing the narrow width of the corridor and not knowing what might be lurking inside those holes, you take your first step into the secondary chambers of the dungeons.

You bolt down the corridor as fast as your feet can take you. Your mad dash is greeted by the sound of metal spears rocketing out of the wall — each spear trying to impale you as you run.

(Roll a six-sided die. If you score 4 or more, you have succeeded in avoiding the volleys of spears, and made it to the other side, where another portal awaits. If, however, you scored 3 or less, lose TWO Health Grades).

- If you survived, turn to **62**

40

Suddenly, the door bursts open and a huge torrent of water, almost like a river, hits you with force. You are rocked by the current as it sends you down and through so many corridors that you lose count, not to mention your bearing.

It is then that you hear the voice of the wizard. "So, you decided to have a swim in the river of memory — a rather foolish pastime, as your memory is now being wiped, I'm afraid."

(Yes, all of your memories, along with all the items and spells in your inventory, will disappear. Now, you will have a chance to begin again, and hopefully, save the princess this time. Good luck!).

- Turn to **56**

41

You cast the RUST spell and watch as it eats away the metal bars of the gate in moments. Beyond, lies a gloomy chamber with dank walls. Huge curtains of cobwebs hang from the vaulted ceiling above.

You cautiously step inside, fingers wrapped around the hilt of your sword.

- Now, Warrior, turn to **86**

42

You wander aimlessly through the maze for what seems an age, but are unable to find a way out. Finally, you hear the disappointed voice of Arudus in your ears.

"You should be more wary, Warrior. Sometimes the very walls and passages of this dungeon can shift around you. A maze is a dangerous place if you do not have a plan for getting out again. But, despite your mishap here, you have impressed me, and I will offer you a chance at redemption."

(Roll a six-sided die. If you roll either a 1 or a 6, you earn mercy from the wizard. If you roll anything else, you will be lost forever in this shifting maze).

- If you earned the wizard's mercy and a second chance, turn to **107**

43

{*} You answer correctly, and the door simply opens without fuss or incident, which makes for a nice change! You follow several corridors, again without any issue. This lack of trouble is starting to make you feel uncomfortable, and puts you on edge. You find another winding staircase and follow it down.

- Now, Warrior, turn to **103**

44

The robed figure cracks his knuckles and you see two ruby-red eyes glowing beneath the hood of his black robe.

"I can hear a tongue wagging, but surely no brains are in that head of yours. That is the wrong answer!"

He clicks his fingers, and you fall through the floor — and keep falling! It is then that you hear the robed figure's voice. "Welcome to the Pit of Forever!"

You fall, and continue falling, and will do so forever.

(You are as good as dead, and for you, Warrior, the challenge has ended! For you, it's Game Over, I'm afraid! Better luck next time).

45

The robed figure cracks his knuckles, and you see two ruby-red eyes glowing beneath the hood of his black robe.

"I can hear a tongue wagging, but surely no brains are in that head of yours. That is the wrong answer."

He clicks his fingers, and a monstrous figure emerges from the rubble and shadows around you. You are face-to-face with a Shadow Golem.

(If you have the KNIGHT spell, you can cast it and it will fight the Golem. If you do not have the spell, the Golem kills you on the spot. If that is the case, you are dead, and for you, Warrior, the challenge has ended).

However, if you do cast the spell, in the chaos of the fighting, you watch as the shifting passages change. You see an exit and make a break for it, but during your escape your legs get injured, smashed by a shifting doorway. (Drop your Health Grade down to RED).

- If you are still alive, you are free of the maze - turn to **60**

46

You have found a rare moment to rest. (While here, your life force returns to GREEN).

Using this time, you check over your inventory. (Remove any items that you no longer need and generally sort yourself out. Hey, reader, it might also be a good time to get a cup of tea and a snack before carrying on).

When you decide to leave, you see two doors. Which do you take?

- Once refreshed, you take the door on the left - turn to **81**
- Once refreshed, you take the door on the right - turn to **164**

47

{*} The old crone hides her face behind her ragged cloak, but her cackling, unhinged tone describes her just as well.

"So," she hisses, "Arudus must be scraping the barrel with you."

She hobbles over to a large chest and opens it to display several objects — a blank parchment, a pot of honey, a rat carving, a stale cake, a full wine skin, and a compass.

"'You can take one item and one item only, but be warned — some of these items are totally useless, while some are not... so, choose wisely...."

- After making your choice, you continue - turn to **60**

48

"Very wise," states the robed sorcerer, peering intently at you as though he can see into your very soul. "Listen close. One chance and one alone do you get! My riddle is this:

I have one and you have one. So do the woods, fields, streams and seas, the fish, beasts and crops and everything else in this revolving world."

What is your answer?

- Sleep - turn to **104**
- Hunger - turn to **44**
- Shadow - turn to **154**
- Soul - turn to **92**

49

You are either a great athlete, a demi-god in disguise, or just plain crazy.

(Roll a six-sided die).

- If you score a 1 or a 2, you succeed in getting across the pit - turn to **98**
- If you score anything else, you fall short, and drop headlong into the pit - turn to **151**

50

You open the door and venture out cautiously. Ahead, are three paths. You take the left, its twisted trail leading you into a ghostly area. Countless traps, swinging axes, and other devices move all around you.

It is then that you hear the stern voice of Arudus. "Brave Warrior, you have stumbled upon the Trap Gauntlet, a series of rather nasty trap rooms. There is no way back, only forward. You must survive the Test of Blades to continue. Good luck, and pray that fortune is with you. Oh, and bear in mind the magical hexes of this room forbid healing and the use of spells."

With that, the voice of the wizard fades away, leaving you with only the frantic beating of your own heart and the metallic whirl of steel blades as they cut through the air.

As you take another step, the ghostly fog of the chamber fades away to reveal a narrow bridge with a sheer, never-ending chasm on either side. Swinging axes whirl from one side of the chamber to the other. You must cross the bridge and avoid the axes to reach the open portal on the other side.

(Roll one six-sided die. If you score 3 or less, you manage to avoid the swinging axes and cross the bridge to the open portal. Otherwise, a blade slices you open and sends you into the void).

- If you survived, turn to **39**

51

You cast the RAT spell and a magical rodent comes to life. It bites your arm so viciously, that blood pours out and over its fangs. Suddenly, it bolts away and you give chase, following it and the trail of your blood out of the maze and back to the winch. (Your Health Grade is now on RED).

- Now, Warrior, turn to **60**

52

You are almost at the exit portal when a rotting paw clamps down hard on your shoulder. You shrug it off, but another grabs your arm and then your legs. In a few seconds, they are all over you, and you feel the first bite of razor-sharp teeth.

(You are as good as dead, and for you, Warrior, the challenge has ended! For you, it's Game Over, I'm afraid! Better luck next time).

53

Up ahead, lie three paths. You take the right. Its twisted trail leads onwards and soon you enter a damp area. There, you find a pile of skeletal remains in the centre, all burned and black. Clutched in a charred skeletal hand is a corked bottle. Taking it, you find a small parchment inside. Opening the bottle and parchment reveals an incantation. Reading it aloud, you wonder what will happen, but nothing does, until Arudus speaks.

"Well, that's an odd spell to cast now. I didn't know that you had it in you... That little incantation has recalled the magic you have spent. You may recover any spell that you have already used, so choose wisely..."

With that, the wizard's voice fades and you carry on.

- Now, Warrior, turn to **100**

54

The enchanted door handle strikes your hand again, firing one of its bolts at you with force. The bolt stabs you in the arm and you fight the urge to howl out in pain. (Lose ONE Health Grade).

Taking a moment, you try to answer the riddle again.

"That was a wrong answer! You have one chance left!" the door handle replies.

- Take your last chance to open the door - turn to **4**

55

You carry the book over to a desk for her. There is an unlit lantern there, but the little fairy says something in a whisper, causing it to light up.

"Look at this," she says, opening the book and pointing at an engraving of a hideous, half-human creature. "It's a ghoul bear. Such beasts are vile and fearsome, but they move slowly and are very stupid. It is possible to stay one step ahead of them if you hold your nerve."

She closes the book and you wonder why she has told you this. Could she know something about what lies ahead on the next level?

"Remember this," she adds, "in general, courage and quick thinking are worth more than brute strength. I have time to teach you one spell. Which will it be — KNIGHT, ESCAPE, AGILITY or IRONWILL?"

(Remember, you cannot possess more than three spells at any time).

Bidding the fairy, Asphodel, farewell, you continue on your way and out through a door in the back of the library.

- Now, Warrior, turn to **11**

56

You have one chance to save you skin and your memory.

(Roll a six-sided die. If you roll a 1 or a 6, you only manage to free yourself from the river. If you scored anything else, return to section 1, and as your adventure will begin again, decide whether you want to or not).

- If you were lucky and scored a 1 or a 6, turn to **120**
- If you scored anything else, turn to **1**

57

As you step through the door, a giant astral hand grabs you and launches you into the never-ending abyss. You will be lost forever!

(For you, Warrior, the challenge has ended! For you, it's Game Over, I'm afraid! Better luck next time).

58

{*} The tunnel in which you find yourself is quite narrow and slopes down into the fetid depths of the dungeon below. You arrive at a door on your left.

- If you open the door, turn to **50**
- If you carry on down the tunnel, turn to **70**

59

You hurl the joint of fresh meat into the farthest corner of the cave. They take the scent and make for it, leaving you with a clean run to the exit portal.

- Now, Warrior, turn to **125**

60

In the centre of the floor, there is a hole, over which a winch stands — it appears to be the way down to the level below. Opposite the portal through which you entered, is the word... MAZE... carved with magically-burning letters upon the keystone above a wide archway.

- If you want to winch yourself down to the next level, turn to **27**
- If you want to explore the maze first, turn to **21**

61

You draw your sword and charge at the bony beast.

(Roll a six-sided die. If you score 4 or higher, you manage to defeat the beast, but in combat your sword shatters and you will have to use the Ogre's thigh bone as your weapon from here on out. If, however, you scored 3 or less, the beast swipes at you with bony clawed hands and kills you. If that is the case, you are dead, and for you, Warrior, the challenge has ended! For you, it's Game Over, I'm afraid! Better luck next time).

- If you survive, turn to **111**

62 - 63

62

You step through the portal and find yourself in a room with a chequered floor. Each square of the grid has a separate letter on it.

As you look at the grid, the voice of the wizard booms overhead. "Spell your way out."

It takes you a moment to understand the clue, before stepping onto the letters **E**, **X**, and **I**. You need to make a leap to reach the letter **T**, and what you hope will be the way out.

(Roll a six-sided die. If you score 3 or less, you successfully reach the letter **T**, and the exit portal opens and for you the Gauntlet is over. If, however, you score 4 or more, you miss the letter and the floor falls away beneath you, sending you plummeting downwards. If this is the case, you are dead, and for you, Warrior, the challenge has ended! For you, it's Game Over, I'm afraid! Better luck next time).

- If you survived, turn to **36**

63

There is no time now for escape or to perform any other action for that matter. The mined chamber explodes and the last thing that you see are your arms and legs flying off in front of you.

(You are dead, and for you, Warrior, the challenge has ended! For you, it's Game Over, I'm afraid! Better luck next time).

64

{*} You pick the lock easily enough and get through it with barely minutes to spare. You are halfway across the chamber when the bomb goes off, but you are unharmed. In this room, you find a table with a small cask of ale and a pork pie. You take both items and push on.

- Now Warrior, turn to **145**

65

You use the compass to keep your bearings as you make your way back through the maze. However, instead of finding the way out, you unexpectedly arrive at an alcove, where a black-cloaked man sits upon a granite throne. Above him, on the wall hangs an inverted iron horseshoe.

"Some say it's unlucky!" the cloaked figure says, taking it down and handing it to you.

It makes your compass spin wildly — a magnet! It's no wonder that you got lost following it here!

"The attraction to the flame of evil, some would call it," suggests the robed stranger, "but, little moth, I might let you go if you can answer my riddle!"

What will you do?

- If you want to attempt to answer the riddle, turn to **48**
- If you want to make a run for it, turn to **135**

66 - 68

66

You cast the KNIGHT spell, and a magical, spectral knight appears and begins to fight the beast. This offers you a chance to escape. You bolt down the corridor and out of sight. As you make your escape, you trip and fall badly, hurting your leg. (Lose ONE Health Grade).

- You limp off and carry on - turn to **111**

67

One of the goblins stabs its rusty dagger into your thigh. (Lose ONE Health Grade). To add insult to injury, the bread is so stale and mouldy, that it has become worm food and is inedible.

- Now, Warrior, turn to **127**

68

"WHAT?" booms the voice of Arudus, whose astral projection now appears before you. "You'll have to try and be a bit bolder than that. The only way is onward — there is no turning back for a TRUE hero! I will not tolerate such a cowardly retreat. As penalty for such craven behaviour, you will lose that which is most precious. Now go!"

(Lose ONE Health Grade).

- Turn to **37**

69

The voice of Arudus magically booms overhead. "Remember, we were hoping that you would become a true hero for the people of the realm. This dungeon challenge was to test of your heroic nature and your guile. A true hero never leaves an innocent in distress. In this case, that innocent was the Princess that you were tasked with freeing. Because you have come this far and have impressed me much, a chance at redemption I shall offer you — by wiping your memory and allowing you to take the dungeon challenge again."

(Your memory has been wiped, along with all of your items and the spells in your inventory. You have a chance to begin again and hopefully save the Princess this time. Good luck!).

- Now, Warrior, turn to **1**

70

The tunnel ends in a chamber of rough-hewn masonry blocks. There is no right-hand wall, but as you move towards it, a sudden and violent tremor nearly rocks you off of your feet. A shower of dust falls from a widening crack in the far wall.

- If you try to run for the door, turn to **123**
- If you wait for the quake to subside, turn to **94**

71

You decide to try and sneak past.

(Roll a six-sided die. If you rolled 3 or less, you have managed to slip through the room unnoticed. If you rolled 4 or more, you have been spotted).

- If you rolled 3 or less, turn to **73**
- If you rolled 4 or more, turn to **156**

72

You step through the right-hand portal and are transported to a dark cave. You cautiously move forward through the gloom.

Suddenly, a torch flares, reflecting on a tall, armoured figure, who marches towards you! Through the figure's open visor, grins a ghastly skull.

It is clearly preparing to attack!

- If you use the crossbow, turn to **157**
- If you use the meat, turn to **159**
- If you use the horn, turn to **79**
- If you have the KNIGHT spell, turn to **12**

73

You arrive at a long, draughty chamber. As you enter, you see a nun kneeling and praying just a few paces away, with her back to you. Hearing you, she stops, stands, and turns. It is then that you see it — a huge sword in her left hand and beads in her right. She raises her sword and slices out at you!

(If you have the SHIELD spell, you can use it, but you will still lose ONE Health Grade. Without this spell, the sword-wielding nun's blow inflicts the loss of TWO Health Grades).

- If you survive, turn to **8**

74

(The filled bottle counts as ONE item).

"Drink it at ANY time," says the old man. "It will give you one use of ANY spell — even one you have never heard of."

Suddenly, a rainbow appears above him and he vanishes.

- Now, Warrior, turn to **126**

75

As you enter the dark shadows ahead of you, you see a Troll snoozing there and blocking your way.

(Roll a six-sided die. On a 3 or less, you manage to sneak past without waking the Troll. On a 4 or more, the disgruntled and rather annoyed Troll smashes you into the cave wall, choking the life out of you. If this is the case, then for you, Warrior, the challenge has ended! For you, it's Game Over, I'm afraid! Better luck next time).

- If you scored 3 or less, you may continue - turn to **109**

76

"Not a bad choice," admits Arudus. "The STEALTH spell makes you almost totally silent and invisible to creatures with normal vision, but it only lasts a short while, so don't idle about once you have cast it."

(Make sure you have the spell in mind, by writing it down).

Get ready to begin your quest!

- Now, Warrior, turn to **20**

77

You have entered a combat room and there is blood-stained sawdust strewn across the floor. Through the single door ahead, clanks the armoured Golem Guardian of Level 2, blocking an exit portal. Raising his broadsword, the Golem challenges you for the password.

- If you have the password, turn to **80**
- If you do not have the password, turn to **96**

78

You cast the spell and fly across the room like a shadow, ducking right between the barbarian's legs without him noticing you. As you pass beneath the brute, you seize the opportunity to help yourself to his small coin purse. (You have gained 20 Gold Coins).

Dropping the coin purse into your satchel, you slip out of the room silently.

- Turn to **73**

79

You place the horn to your lips and blow furiously. A great sound echoes through the cave, but nothing else happens, and the enemy continues its deadly advance.

(You are doomed unless you have the KNIGHT spell and cast it now. If not, you are dead, and for you, Warrior, the challenge has ended! For you, it's Game Over, I'm afraid! Better luck next time).

- If you have the spell, cast it now
 - turn to **12**

80

That was a bad decision. There was never a password! Cheats and fools never prosper in these dungeons.

(For you, Warrior, the challenge has ended! For you, it's Game Over, I'm afraid! Better luck next time).

81

You enter a chamber with only one exit. Reaching the exit would be easy, except for the well-armed guard at the door. You have no choice but to fight.

(Roll a six-sided die. If you score 4 or more, you have bested the guard. Anything else causes the loss of ONE Health Grade. If you score 3 or less, you injured the guard, distracting them just long enough for you to reach the exit).

- Now, Warrior, turn to **84**

82

At the end of a short passage, you find a room from which a stairwell descends into the dungeon's depths.

The voice of the great wizard whispers on the breeze, and into your mind. "Brave warrior, to complete this level of the dungeon, a princess you must find and save — find the Princess!"

You remember his words and head back to the staircase. Halfway down, you find a door in the side wall. There, a small stairwell continues down for a few more feet.

What will you do?

- Open the Door - turn to **138**
- Continue downwards - turn to **53**

83

"Thank you, good sir," he wheezes in a reedy voice as you help him down.

Clutching a gnarled, walking stick, he hobbles over to the roots of the tree and points to three pools in the rock there.

"Go on, go on," he cackles. "The Three Fountains of Yggdrasill, or the World Tree in the Common Tongue."

Looking at them, they seem like nothing more than dirty puddles, but the old man pushes a leather water bottle into your hands and insists that you fill it. "Go on! It'll do you a power of good."

But which fountain will you fill the bottle from?

- The First - turn to **13**
- The Second - turn to **33**
- The Third - turn to **91**

84

DANGER! This cave is swarming with Zombified Vampire Bats. Although totally blind and deaf, their sense of smell is unmatched and they have your scent. They come flying towards you. There is only one of you and ten of them, and they block your route to the only obvious exit portal.

What will you do?

- Use the horn and try for the door
  - turn to **52**
- Try the crossbow if you have it
  - turn to **130**
- Use the meat, if you have it
  - turn to **59**

85

The Goblins rant and cry out in a language that you do not understand. They run around the table, aiming to cut you off. You can see a door at the far end of the hall.

What will you do?

- If you decide to run straight for the door, turn to **127**
- If you risk pausing long enough to snatch up one of the bread crusts, turn to **67**

86

You step through the iron gate and unwittingly trigger a trap. The floor suddenly breaks away beneath you and you begin to fall. Turning your head, you see a pit of spikes below.

(Roll a six-sided die. If you score 3 or less, you have managed to grab the sides of the hole. You then shimmy yourself along its edge to safety. Anything else and you have died, and your challenge is over).

- If you survived, turn to **129**

87

About ten metres into the watery passage, you spot a small door set back into the rock wall. You open it, only to be blasted though a portal into a square chamber. The chamber is empty except for three exits. The exit to the left is open, but the one in the middle and the other to the right are both blocked by heavy portcullises. Glancing upwards, you see a wooden lever, which might control the two portcullises, but it is beyond your reach.

- If you take the left exit, turn to **18**
- If you try something else, turn to **9**

88

{*} As you leave, you notice something lying behind a block of stone in the corner. It is a clay jar — most likely left behind by the dungeon's builders aeons ago. Opening the jar, you find a scroll with the spell KNIGHT upon it.

(Once cast, a warrior will appear and fight in your place, taking any damage dealt. Make sure you have the spell in mind, by writing it down).

You step through the hidden portal.

- Now, Warrior, turn to **109**

89

Just because they are small, does not mean that Goblins are pushovers. They move with inhuman speed and agility, and soon they are all around you. Unarmed, you fall under a hail of rusty metal, pierced like a bloody pincushion.

(Next time, remember that discretion is often the better option!).

90

There is no time for escape. You bolt towards the left door, but it is too late. The mines explode and you are blown into a hundred small pieces, each one smaller than the last.

(You are dead, and for you, Warrior, the challenge has ended! For you, it's Game Over, I'm afraid! Better luck next time).

91

"An odd choice, but, oh well... the Pool of Fate!"

(The filled bottle counts as one item. You can drink it ANY time that you need to make a dice roll. It enables you to automatically succeed on any single dice roll, but it can only be used once).

Suddenly, a rainbow appears over the old man and he vanishes.

- Now, Warrior, turn to **126**

92

The robed figure cracks his knuckles and you see two, ruby-red eyes glowing beneath the hood of his black robe.

"I can hear a tongue wagging, but surely no brains are in that head of yours. That is the wrong answer!"

He clicks his fingers, and a monstrous figure emerges from the rubble and shadows around you. You are face to face with a Shadow Golem.

(If you have the KNIGHT spell, you cast it and it fights the Golem. If you do not have the spell, the Golem kills you on the spot. If that is the case, you are dead, and for you, Warrior, the challenge has ended! For you, it's Game Over, I'm afraid! Better luck next time. However, if you do have the spell, in the chaos of the fighting you see the shifting passages change once more).

You spy the exit and make a break for it, but during your escape, your legs are injured, smashed by a shifting doorway. (Drop your Health Grade down to RED).

- If you are still alive, you make it out of the maze - turn to **60**

93

The robed figure cracks his knuckles and you see two, ruby-red eyes glowing beneath the hood of his black robe.

"I can hear a tongue wagging, but surely no brains are in that head of yours. That is the wrong answer!"

He clicks his fingers, and you begin to age. The years fly by in seconds, until you die, decay, and crumble to dust.

(You are dead, and for you, Warrior, the challenge has ended! For you, it's Game Over, I'm afraid! Better luck next time).

94

You fold your arms over your head and crouch down until the room stops shaking. When you look up, you see that an eerie change has befallen the far wall. It now resembles a monstrous face, with buttresses for jowls and arched vaults in place of eyebrows. Several masonry blocks part to form a parody of a mouth.

"I am Boulderax!" it booms. "Answer my riddle or be crushed in these jaws of rock."

You try to hide your fear.

"Speak on," you declare. "Ask your riddle. I will answer."

Boulderax speaks:
"What is it that is blind with an eye in its head, but the race of mankind its use cannot spare; spends all its life in clothing the dead, but always itself is naked and bare?"

What is your answer?

- A Pen - turn to **14**
- A Coffin - turn to **144**
- A Needle - turn to **115**
- A Grave - turn to **22**

95

You cast the HAMMER spell, and your fist begins to glow. You draw your sword and take a swing, but the skeletal beast rips it out of your hand and flings it into the darkness. Your sword is now lost. The beast comes at you again, but before the Ogre has a chance to do anything, you hit it with a warhammer-like blow, taking its huge skull clean off its bony shoulders. Your eyes follow the skull as it flies through the air, crashing into the wall and splintering in a shower of fragments.

- You pick up an Ogre's thigh bone as a weapon, and push on - turn to **111**

96

This really is not very promising, is it? You have completely blown it this time. The Golem runs you through with his broadsword. You are most definitely dead, and for you, Warrior, the challenge has ended! For you, it's Game Over, I'm afraid! Better luck next time.

97

"You have gained the RUST spell. An odd choice," admits the wizard, "but I'm sure, however, that you will find a use for it."

(Make sure you have the spell in mind, by writing it down).

You leave the arena.

- Now, Warrior, turn to **145**

98

You make the leap, relying more on dumb luck than anything else. You succeed in jumping, yes, but the landing is a different matter. As you crash down, you hear an unsettling crack in your ankle. That cannot be good! (Lose ONE Health Grade)

- Now, Warrior, turn to **34**

99

You take the golden goblet and fill it from the fountain's basin. As you begin to drink, you hear Arudus in your mind.

"You chose impurely, for a hero does not go looking for gold, nor reputation or glory... such things end poorly! As such, your choice of gold has led to a dire ending for you and your quest, for the gold has poisoned the water and you will be a mere memory of this dungeon by the time I finish speaking. Goodbye, Warrior!"

(You will be dead soon, and for you, the challenge has ended! For you, it's Game Over, I'm afraid! Better luck next time).

100

{*} You head along a passage, which turns sharply to the right. At the bend in the passage, there is a padlocked, iron gate set into the left-hand wall.

What will you do?

- If you have the RUST spell and wish to cast it, turn to **41**
- If you have the HAMMER spell and wish to cast it, turn to **139**
- If you have a chisel, turn to **143**
- If you wish to carry on down the passage, turn to **128**

101

"Be as quiet as you can," the serving girl warns you once you have removed her gag. "That 'sack' over there, is not a sack at all, but a hideous, and rather large, Boggart, who caught me earlier. It is asleep now, but I believe it intends to torture me further when it wakes up."

"More likely it intends to roast and eat you," you suggest dryly, glancing at the various braziers.

When you take a closer look, you see that the shapeless lump is, indeed, a Boggart, wrapped in a sackcloth skirt. Flies buzz around it as it sleeps.

- If you have the crucifix, and wish to use it, turn to **150**
- If you have the SLEEP spell, and wish to cast it, turn to **134**
- If you kick the Boggart awake, turn to **31**

102

You bolt towards the right-hand door and dive through it. As your body passes through the door's threshold, you narrowly miss a guillotine-like portcullis, which clangs down behind you.

You now find yourself in a dark, narrow corridor, which you feel your way along for several minutes. Its twisted trail leads past countless rooms, but soon you see firelight up ahead and make for it, entering a time-worn area. A huge, hammer-wielding Barbarian stands guard in the centre, along with dozens of what may have once been human skeletons, who now surround him.

Quickly, you duck low behind a pillar and survey the chamber. You see a large, wooden door behind the Barbarian — most likely the exit. You must simply succeed in getting past him.

What will you do?

- If you know the STEALTH spell and want to cast it, turn to **78**
- If you try to sneak past without attracting his attention, turn to **71**
- If you decide to fight him, trusting to your sword, turn to **156**

103

At the bottom of the stairwell is a small chamber, filled with straw. As you feel your way through it, you use your fingers to guide the way. Rummaging around, you discover a circular shield decorated with a single blue eye. You also find a long bow and a quiver full of arrows. (You may, if you like, take all of these items with you).

Clambering out of the sea of straw, you soon realise that you are in a cavern. A shallow stream of swiftly-running water flows through it, before forming a waterfall at the farthest end. The stream enters through a low archway and this appears to present the only possible exit. On a rock, by the water's edge, you find a small loaf of bread, which you can eat.

- Ducking your head, you wade into the stream - turn to **87**

104

The robed figure cracks his knuckles, and you see two, ruby-red eyes glowing beneath the hood of his black robe.

"I can hear a tongue wagging, but surely no brains are in that head of yours. That is the wrong answer!"

He clicks his fingers and your entire body bursts instantly into flames.

(You are dead, and for you, Warrior, the challenge has ended! For you, it's Game Over, I'm afraid! Better luck next time).

105

You step through the door and unwittingly into a portal. You find yourself in a town of some sort, standing in front of a tavern. From the outside, it looks rustic, enchanting, and well-maintained. It is near impossible to see through the closed windows, but the happiness and joy emanating from within can be felt outside. You see a sign overhead that reads 'The Big Red Cocke'.

As you enter the tavern, through the old, wooden door, you are welcomed by a pleasant atmosphere and cheerful singing. The landlady, Bursa Blackhand, is a little preoccupied, but still manages to welcome you with a smile.

The walls are swarming with paintings, some of which are most likely notable locals and the other ones probably of happy customers. The tavern itself is packed. Merchants and tourists seem to be the primary clientele here, which often means great company. Several, long tables are occupied by happy, excited groups of people, some dancing on tables, while others cheer them on with clapping and yelling. The other, smaller tables are also occupied by people who clearly enjoy each other's company, although, they seem to be strangers who have met here. Most of the stools at the bar are occupied, but nobody seems to mind more company.

You have heard rumours about this tavern. Supposedly, it is famous for something, but you cannot remember what. Judging by the music and how many people are dancing, it must be the musicians who have just started playing. You manage to find a seat and prepare for what will undoubtedly be a great evening, that is, until Bursa comes over with an ale in hand.

"I'm sorry, luv, you're in the wrong book! This here is Broodhaven... you know, the town found in Dr. Graham A. Wilson's gamebook, 'Rise Of The Ancients: Bruidd.' Now, have an ale on me and drink up, and when you're done, hop back over to your own book. You most likely have some quest or the like to complete. Well, bye then, deary!"

(For more information about this gamebook, skip to the very back of this book).

- When you have finished your ale, you step through the portal, and back into Warrior - turn to **25**

106

Your choice appears foolish. This chamber has four exits, but each one is barred by an iron portcullis.

(Unless you have the ESCAPE spell, you will have to wait here until you die. For you the challenge has ended. It's Game Over, I'm afraid! Better luck next time).

- Turn to **112**

107

"Prepare to be transported!" you hear Arudus boom in your ears.

It is then that you feel the wizard's giant, astral hand grab you and hurl you into the darkness of the dungeon. The next instant, you are back in the antechamber of the great wizard, the same chamber that started this very dungeon quest. (Any items or spells that you have collected are gone).

"This is your one and only second chance! However, my mercy isn't free! A price must be paid!"

(This time, you start the adventure on AMBER, and may not collect any food until you reach Level 2).

"Now you are armed with something more powerful than a sword — knowledge!"

Do you want to try the dungeon adventure again?

- Now, Warrior, turn to **1**

108

You step through the portal and find yourself falling towards a bottomless pit of black water.

(There is no escape, unless, of course, you have the ESCAPE spell. If you do, you may cast it now. If not, you are dead, and for you, Warrior, the challenge has ended! For you, it's Game Over, I'm afraid! Better luck next time).

- You cast the ESCAPE spell - turn to **120**

109

You have not gone far, when you come to a dingy, little room, where an ugly crone stands mumbling to herself as she stirs her bubbling cauldron. You are thinking about sneaking past when she turns around and sees you.

What will you do?

- Will you run across to the exit portal on the other side of the room? - turn to **136**
- Will you stop and talk? - turn to **47**

110

You take the golden goblet and fill it from the fountain's basin. As you begin to drink, you pick up the sense of something — hemlock. The water is poisoned! You spit out the water, but are a little too late as the poison hits your body like a venomous snake bite. (You have lost TWO Health Grades).

You hear Arudus in your mind. "Well, that was eventful! Your choice almost cost you that which you hold dearest — your life! A warrior does not require rewards such as silver, for a true warrior's reward is a just cause!"

- Now, Warrior, turn to **11**

111

"DANGER! This Chamber is mined and on a very short fuse! You literally have seconds to decide what to do. Now would be a good time to do something — anything!"

You scan the room as quickly as you can and spot two exits to the left and right of you.

Which will you choose?

- You take the exit on the right - turn to **119**
- You take the exit on the left - turn to **90**

112

You make for the right-hand door as fast as you can, but you are a few seconds too late, and the bombed floor explodes, taking the room with it. You are blown through the right-hand doorway by the force of the blast. Then, the floor of the next chamber gives way, and you fall hard, sprawling on the hard-packed, sand floor of a dimly lit cave. Apart from the bones of a few unlucky heroes and adventurers, the cave is empty. However, you get the impression that this is not a good place to linger.

There are two exits, both of which appear dark and foreboding. Which will you choose?

- The Right-hand exit - turn to **106**
- The Left-hand exit - turn to **75**

113

The gagged serving girl was trying to tell you something, but foolishly, you decided not to remove her gag. The next thing you know, you are seized around the throat by a vile arm. A hideous Boggart has you in a stranglehold. You struggle, but cannot break free.

The last thing you see as it chokes the life out of you is the serving girl running off in terror. You managed to rescue an innocent, so maybe you did not die in vain.

(For you, Warrior, the challenge has ended. For you, it's Game Over, I'm afraid! Better luck next time).

114

Whatever made you think that you could run that sort of distance in under ten seconds? Anyway, you are now the fastest corpse in the dungeon graveyard.

(For you, Warrior, the challenge has ended! For you, it's Game Over, I'm afraid! Better luck next time).

115

"Correct!" Boulderax states dryly. "You may pass."

A magical portal emerges in front of his rocky jowls. You are about to take the portal on the right side of the room, when Boulderax draws your attention to another, previously hidden portal that has just materialised in the opposite wall.

"I'd advise you to go by that route," he proposes.

- If you stick to your original choice, turn to **28**
- If you choose to take the portal that Boulderax recommends, turn to **88**

116

As you walk along the corridor, you trigger a trap. A portcullis slams down behind you and a huge swinging axe is let loose. The size of the axe suggests that if it hits you, there will be no coming back. You will be dead! You follow the arc of the axe, trying to get the timing.

(If you have the SHIELD spell, you may cast it now. If the trap hits when cast, it will inflict the loss of TWO Health Grades, rather than dealing instant death).

You watch for a second or two longer, then make your move.

(Roll a six-sided die. You must score a 3 to dodge the swinging axe).

- If you survive, turn to **11**

117

As you begin to drink, you hear Arudus in your mind. "You chose wisely, for a hero must possess humility and modesty!"

As you begin to drink, you feel a surge pass through your body, and your strength is restored. (Your Health Grade has returned to GREEN).

- Now, Warrior, turn to **11**

118

For the remainder of your life, you will be stuck in the Mirror Symmetry Realm. You are as good as dead, and for you, Warrior, the challenge has ended! For you, it's Game Over, I'm afraid! Better luck next time.

- Now, Warrior, turn to **121**

119

You step through the exit only to find yourself being used as a ball, tossed by many astral hands, who are basically playing catch with your body as they fling you every which way possible through the darkness. You are literally bounced a few times, before the astral hands drop you like a sack of spuds on the dungeon floor below. (Lose ONE Health Grade).

- Now, Warrior, turn to **100**

120

{*} (Well done. You have reached Level 3 of the Dungeon Challenge. Take this opportunity to discard any items that you no longer wish to carry).

On a stone table in front of you is a joint of raw meat, a brass horn, and a loaded crossbow. (You may take a maximum of TWO objects).

There are two exit portals to choose from...

- The left portal - turn to **108**
- The right portal - turn to **72**

121

You have fallen into a symmetry trap, stuck in the mirror dimension. What are you going to do?

(You are as good as dead, and for you, Warrior, the challenge has ended! For you, it's Game Over, I'm afraid! Better luck next time).

- Now, Warrior, turn to **118**

122

You charge through the shimmering exit portal and find yourself at one end of a long, narrow corridor. At the far end, at least a hundred metres away, there is another exit portal. However, hanging above your head is a huge bomb with its fuse burning brightly. On the floor beside you is a bucket of water. Glancing quickly at the fuse, you estimate that it has less than ten seconds left to burn.

What will you do?

- Sprint for the exit - turn to **114**
- Use the bucket of water - turn to **147**

123

You decide to make a break for it and run for the door before the next quake brings the tunnel down on top of you.

(Roll a six-sided die. If you score 3 or less, then you reach the door and pass through it safely. But if you score 4 or more, you are unlucky enough to be struck by a huge falling piece of debris, instantly crushing the life out of you. You are dead. For you, Warrior, the challenge has ended. For you, it's Game Over, I'm afraid! Better luck next time).

- If you score 3 or less, turn to **94**

124

You decide to take a quick drink, noticing that on the side of the basin there are three goblets — Gold, Silver and Bronze. You have a feeling that if you wish to take a drink, you will need to pick the correct goblet. A wrong choice might prove fatal.

So, which goblet do you choose?

- The Gold - turn to **99**
- The Silver - turn to **110**
- The Bronze - turn to **117**

125

As you step through it, the portal closes in behind you, blocking your retreat. You start to wonder if you have made the right choice, for there is no going back now. You push on for a while through the near darkness and soon come to a cavernous chamber with walls of unworked stone. A gnarled tree grows out of the rock here. In its upper boughs, sits an old man with grey-streaked hair, his dirty cloak snagged in the branches.

- If you call up to him, turn to **10**
- If you continue on your way, turn to **126**

126

Your way is blocked by a high stone wall, which runs across the centre of this chamber. It is topped with iron spikes and there is no way to climb it. There is a sign attached to the wall, which simply reads: JERICHO.

What will you do now?

- If you have the crossbow, turn to **153**
- If you have the horn, turn to **23**

127

The Goblins chase you around the table and out through the door. They pursue you down various twisting, narrow corridors, baying for your blood, and slightly gaining on you with every turn. Eventually, they give up the chase.

You head deeper into the dungeon, until you reach a large round chamber.

- Now, Warrior, turn to **155**

128

Walking down the passage, you soon find that it splits into two paths. The right one is a dead end, so you take the left. Its twisted trail leads past pillaged rooms and soon you enter a ragged area. Spiderwebs cover everything. Large figures seem to be wrapped in the same web. Through the blankets of thick webbing, you see an exit portal shimmering at the far left of the chamber, with a stone arched exit opposite it on the far right.

As you step further inside, you hear the sound of many feet on flagstone. You turn, only to be confronted by a huge Spider, with its fangs poised and dripping with poison. You have no choice but to fight your way out. (Roll a six-sided die).

- If you rolled a score of 3 or less, your attacks against the Spider prove pointless and you lose ONE Health Grade, but manage to make a break for the stone archway - turn to **16**
- If you rolled a 4 or more, you have killed the Giant Spider and done so in style. You bolt away through the shimmering exit portal - turn to **21**

129

Only a short distance further, along a narrow dim corridor, you pass a fountain and basin set back into an alcove off to the side of the corridor.

- If you stop to drink, turn to **124**
- If you press on along the corridor, turn to **116**

130

You fire your one and only crossbow bolt, to little effect. Yes, you killed one, but there are still nine more coming towards you. A rotting limb seizes you and you feel the piercing of the beast's razor-sharp teeth as they cut into your neck.

(You are dead, and for you, Warrior, the challenge has ended! For you, it's Game Over, I'm afraid! Better luck next time).

131

{*} "I don't know how to thank you," coos the serving girl. "Brave hero, despite my looks, I am no mere serving girl, but am, in fact, Princess Allora! The Boggart kidnapped me from my home many months ago. I'm sure it had some unspeakable fate in store for me if you hadn't come along. Perhaps I can give you some aid or help in your quest in return. I have heard the portal to the next dungeon level is guarded and that a password is needed to open it. I know

131 Continued

nothing of what guards it, but the Boggart did say a word a lot.... Now, what was it? Oh, yes, 'PATNTIBUS'. I think it means 'open' in the Old Tongue."

The princess also gives you a pendant from around her neck. "But that is not all I can do to thank you, brave hero. Please take this also, as a token of my thanks."

The next voice you hear belongs to Arudus. "Well, Allora, you are safe.... My thanks, hero.... You have earned my aid when and if you need it most."

Then a portal opens and the princess steps through it and is gone.

"Brave Warrior," Arudus says, "beyond this chamber is the final test! To become the hero that destiny knows you to be, if you can beat the Dark Lord and find the Crescent Sword, you will have completed my test and become a TRUE hero."

As quickly as it began, the wizard's voice is gone, and you step through the portal, and into the final part of this dungeon challenge.

- Now, Warrior, turn to **120**

132

You find yourself in a chamber with three doors before you. More importantly, hanging over your head there is a huge bomb with its fuse burning brightly. You try the doors, only to find that you will need to pick one of their locks before the bomb explodes. (Roll a six-sided die).

- To open the left door and pick its lock, you need to roll a 1 or a 2 - turn to **19**
- To open the right door and pick its lock, you need to roll a 3 or a 4 - turn to **64**
- To open the middle door and pick its lock, you need to roll a 5 or a 6 - turn to **140**

133

There is no time for escape. You bolt towards the left door, but it is too late — the mines explode and you are blown into a hundred small pieces, each one smaller than the last!

(For you, Warrior, the challenge has ended! For you, it's Game Over, I'm afraid! Better luck next time).

134

You cast the spell, and from out of your fingers, issues forth a shower of dust, raining down upon the boggart's hideous features. It snores even more loudly but does not wake when you shout into its ear, or when you give it a rather strong nudge with your boot. Now, you must free the serving girl, before the spell wears off.

- Now, Warrior, turn to **146**

135

Trusting in your strength, you make a break for it. The robed figure makes no attempt to chase you. Instead, he yawns and simply waves his hand. You jolt up into the air and fly backwards with force to where the cloaked figure sits. It takes you a few seconds to figure out what has just happened — you are dealing with a sorcerer! Great... this is the last thing you needed! (Lose TWO Health Grades, owing to the bone-jarring impact).

"Now," he says, "you aren't going to try that again, are you?"

- You shake your head and agree to answer the riddle - turn to **48**

136

The old crone throws a vial of the cauldron's contents at you, hitting you on the arm and burning you badly. (Lose TWO Health Grades). Seeing you wounded, she gives a mad shriek and chases after you. You waste no time in darting through the exit portal. Despite your wound, you keep running, even after passing through the portal, until you can no longer hear her mad shrieking.

- Turn to **60**

137

You trade your trusty boots for the winged sandals, experiencing a brief twinge of sheer panic as you make a small running take off. However, the winged sandals keep you airborne as you hoped they would. When you reach the far side, the sandals slip off your feet and fly away before you can catch them. Putting your trusty boots back on, you now turn your attention to the chest.

- Now, Warrior, turn to **34**

138

The door creaks open to reveal a long room. You catch a glimpse of rats at the far end, squeaking their protests at the sudden intrusion of your torchlight.

Entering, you see a copper-banded chest about ten metres away. However, there is a five-metre wide pit directly in front of you. You throw in a small stone and it drops for what seems like forever. If you fell in there, you have a feeling that you would be well and truly dead.

What will you do?

- If you try jumping across (you have just enough space for a small run up), turn to **49**
- If you have the winged sandals, turn to **137**
- You decide to turn back, and head down the stairs - turn to **132**

139

You cast the HAMMER spell and watch as your fist begins to glow. The spell has given your right fist the strength of a great war hammer, and even if it only lasts a short time, it will get you past this gate. Swinging your fist, you smash clean through the gate, stepping uneasily into the dank chamber beyond.

- Turn to **86**

140

You step through the door and unwittingly into a portal. You find yourself in a town or city of some sort, standing in front of a tavern. From the outside, it looks folksy, homely, and delightful. Small stones and wooden pillars make up most of the building's outer structure. A sign overhead reads, 'The One Eyed Rat.' It is hard to see through the high windows, but the excitement from within can be felt outside.

As you enter the tavern, through the huge, hard, wooden door, you are welcomed by a sense of home and a feeling of comfort. The bartender is engaged in a conversation, but still manages to welcome you with a friendly nod. It is as lovely inside as it is on the outside. Hard wooden beams support the upper floor and the large candles attached to them. The walls are decorated with mounted animal heads, hides, and small animals. It is clear the owner is an avid hunter, or at least one of the patrons is, and the smells coming from the kitchen indicate that the animals do not go to waste.

The tavern itself is packed. Workers seem to be the primary clientele here, which often means great company. Several long tables are occupied by what seems to be the entire surrounding village. The other, smaller tables are also occupied by people who are probably starting to reach the point of having drunk too much. Most of the stools at the bar are occupied, although nobody seems to mind more company.

140 Continued

You have heard rumours about this tavern. Supposedly it is famous for something, but you cannot remember what for. Although, judging by the warmth and joy radiating throughout the tavern, it is probably the atmosphere that makes this tavern famous.

You manage to find a seat and prepare for what will undoubtedly be a great evening, that is, until the bartender comes over with an ale in hand.

"Oi' mate, you're in the wrong book… 'Jailbreak.' You know, the gamebook written by David Lowrie. Now have an ale on me and drink up, and when you're done, hop back over to your own book. You most likely have some quest or the like to complete. Well, bye then, pal!"

(For more information about this gamebook, skip to the very back of this book).

- Time to head back into your own book and adventure - turn to **132**

141

"So, that's what happened to my wand" says the fairy, Asphodel, as she spies her stolen property. "You, little goblin... stealing my wand! How dare you? Well, if you want to go around stealing things, then you might as well look the part."

With that, she turns you into a magpie. Perhaps she will relent and restore you to human form after a while — a century or two, maybe.

(For you, Warrior, the challenge has ended! For you, it's Game Over, I'm afraid! Better luck next time).

142

You answer, "Sun."

Suddenly, you hear a click, and from above, a cauldron of boiling oil pours down on you, burning you alive.

(You are dead, and for you, Warrior, the challenge has ended! For you, it's Game Over, I'm afraid! Better luck next time).

143

It takes some time and a wound to the hand (lose ONE Health Grade), but you finally open the link of the padlock. Just as you administer the last stroke, the chisel unfortunately snaps, and you must discard it from your inventory. Still, at least you opened the lock.

You swing the gate wide and step into the cold clammy chamber on the other side.

- Turn to **86**

144

Boulderax issues a hollow laugh. "WRONG! Now I shall devour you!"

His massive stone jaws crunch down, but suddenly, an astral hand appears and you are hurled backwards by it, so instead of being crushed to death, you are severely hurt instead. As you land, you hear something break. (Lose ONE Health Grade).

If you survive this, you hear Arudus and the Rock Monster arguing and use this distraction to make a break for it.

- Turn to **36**

145

You follow a small, twisting corridor past pillaged rooms and soon you enter a damp area. The enormous, beastly skeleton of a Mountain Ogre is chained to the wall. You take a moment to look it over, grateful that it is not alive.

As you head towards the exit, however, you hear the sound of bones jangling, and turning to investigate, narrowly manage to avoid a skeletal fist hurtling towards you.

The Skeletal Ogre is now very much alive and blocking the exit!

- If you have the HAMMER spell and wish to use it, turn to **95**
- If you have the KNIGHT spell and wish to use it, turn to **66**
- If you have neither, you must fight the Skeletal Ogre - turn to **61**

146

(You can free the serving girl using either a chisel or a RUST spell. If the former, then you can keep the chisel, although, you lose the spell in the usual way, as, with all spells, they can only be used once).

- If you free the serving girl, turn to **131**
- If you are unable to free her, for whatever reason, you shrug and walk away - turn to **69**

147

You hurl the bucket of water at the huge bomb and the fuse fizzles out. Now you can walk across the room at your leisure to the exit and through it into a large round chamber beyond.

- Now, Warrior, turn to **155**

148

You try to think ahead, and using a splinter of wood found on the floor as a quill, prick your finger and make a map drawn in your own blood as you explore the maze. However, your plan falls short when you try to use the map to find your way out. Even though you have followed the map exactly, you are still lost, and what's worse is the shifting passages of the maze have ensnared you. You have been caught in a symmetry trap.

- Now, Warrior, turn to **121**

149

"DANGER! This Chamber is mined and is on a very short fuse. Now would be a good time to move, don't you think?"

You scan the room as quickly as you can and spot one exit.

(Roll a six-sided die. If you score a 1 or a 6, you make it to the exit in one piece. If you rolled anything else, the bomb explodes and so do you. You are dead, and for you Warrior, the challenge has ended! For you, it's Game Over, I'm afraid! Better luck next time).

- Now, Warrior, turn to **46**

150

The Boggart lets out an inhuman wail as it sleeps, shriveling away before your eyes. Soon, there is nothing left but a pile of dank ash.

You retrieve the crucifix and wipe it clean before going back to the serving girl.

- Now, Warrior, turn to **146**

151

You miss the jump and fall into the pit. The landing hits hard and rocks your whole body. (Lose TWO Health Grades).

"Well, that looked painful!" Arudus' voice booms overhead. "Welcome to the arena. You must face and beat all three of this dungeon's gladiatorial brutes."

(Every time you win, your Health Grade replenishes One Level. Beat all three, and you may claim a reward and leave the arena to carry on your challenge).

(Roll a six-sided die).

Gladiator #1
(To beat this gladiator, you must roll a score of 1 or 2. Anything else loses a Health Grade).

151 Continued

Gladiator #2
(To beat this gladiator, you must roll a score of 3 or 4. Anything else loses a Health Grade).

Gladiator #3
(To beat this gladiator, you must roll a score of 5 or 6. Anything else loses a Health Grade).

"Well done," the wizard booms. "That was a fight to remember. Now, to your prize."

In front of you, three chests appear, each one emblazoned with a golden number.

- You choose Reward 1 - turn to **3**
- You choose Reward 2 - turn to **97**
- You choose Reward 3 - turn to **35**

152

"Very wise," says Arudus, "after all, you might always find food, but magic is hard to come by. Now, which spell will you take?"

- You decide to take the STEALTH spell - turn to **76**
- You decide to take the SHIELD spell - turn to **6**

153

You fire the crossbow's only shot at the wall, but realise, as the bolt rebounds into your chest, that you are doomed.

(You are dead, and for you, Warrior, the challenge has ended! For you, it's Game Over, I'm afraid! Better luck next time).

154

"Hmmmm," you hear from beneath the dark shadowy folds of his robe. "Correct, so you've earned your life, but not your freedom — not yet!"

"That riddle was for my freedom!" you protest.

"Well, I'm changing the rules! If you want to get out of this maze, you'll have to answer another riddle."

You have no choice, and have a hunch that even if you are correct, the rules may change yet again.

"Okay. What is this second riddle?" you enquire.

"This is my riddle:

An eater lacking mouth and even maw; yet trees and beasts to it are daily bread. Well fed, it thrives and shows a lively life, but give it water and you do it dead."

What is your answer?

- A Candle - turn to **26**
- The Abyss - turn to **93**
- Fire - turn to **158**
- Drought - turn to **45**

155

{*} You find yourself in a large, round chamber. Next to a tapestry of some long-forgotten battle stands Arudus.

"Well, you have made it this far in one piece. Now, the time has come to prove your true mettle, beyond simply completing the challenge of the Guild's Dungeon!"

The Great Wizard raises his hand and begins to chant as a portal begins to take shape in the centre of the chamber.

"From this point on, the challenges you face will be harder and more deadly. Remember, that the dungeon you will soon venture back into exists to test the many qualities that a true hero should possess. In addition to quick-wittedness, you must demonstrate bravery, diplomacy, honour, and mercy. These were all virtues that our Great King had in abundance, before the Red Queen dethroned him."

You nod, your jaw set in determination even though your heart is pounding. The Dungeons below the Wizards' Guild have an awesome reputation, and you have heard that many would-be heroes and adventurers have failed to deal with its tests and traps. When Arudus gives you the sword that you lost at the start of this challenge, you see that your hand is steady.

155 Continued - 157

"I am ready" you tell him.

The Great Wizard raises his hand and points to the portal. You take a step closer and pause for a moment.

(If you have any food items that you wish to consume to improve your Health Grade, now is the time).

- When you are ready, step through the portal, and turn to **7**

156

(Roll a six-sided die. If you roll 3 or less, you have fought the barbarian to a stalemate, and seeing you a worthy opponent, he lets you pass. Lose ONE Health Grade. However, if you rolled 4 or more, your attempt to fight the barbarian has fallen short and you have been badly wounded. Lose TWO Health Grades).

- Now, Warrior, turn to **73**

157

You aim the crossbow and fire, but the weapon has no effect. (You are doomed unless you have the KNIGHT spell and you cast it now. If not, you are dead, and for you, Warrior, the challenge has ended! For you, it's Game Over, I'm afraid! Better luck next time).

- If so, cast the spell now, and turn to **12**

158

{*} You answer correctly. The robed figure says nothing. Instead, he clicks his fingers and three chests appear before you.

"Pick a prize, and then go!"

In the 1st chest is a small cask of ale.

In the 2nd chest is a Re-roll Charm, which allows you to re-roll any single failed dice roll, but only once.

In the 3rd chest is an ESCAPE spell.

You collect your prize and run before the robed figure has another riddle come to mind. Now that you have the robed figure's magnetic horseshoe, you can destroy it and finally use the compass to find your way back out of this confusing maze.

- Now, Warrior, turn to **60**

159

You hurl the joint of meat at the enemy. This is a mistake as this monster cares not for food. (You are doomed unless you have the KNIGHT spell and cast it now. If not, you are dead, and for you, Warrior, the challenge has ended! For you, it's Game Over, I'm afraid! Better luck next time).

- If you have the spell, cast it now, and turn to **12**

160

You raise your shield before you. A bright, blue light radiates from its surface as it responds to the threat of the Dark Eye. For a few seconds, Blue fight Black, until there is a loud, splitting and cracking, and the Dark Eye shatters into a thousand pieces. In its wake, the CRIMSON SWORD appears.

"Congratulations!" says Arudus. "You have prevailed and beaten the Dark One, known as Voldrak, as well as recovering the Sword of Heroes and passing my test — a test to see if you are a TRUE hero! But now, your real quest begins...."

**TO BE CONTINUED
IN WARRIOR, BOOK 2...**

161

You cast the SLEEP spell and the brute falls into a slumber. You know the spell will not last long, so you make your move.

(Roll a six-sided die. If you score a 3 or less, you manage to make it around the Cerebus and out through the door. If you score anything else, you waited a little too long and the claws of the beast strike you as you leave. Lose TWO Health Grades).

- If you survive, turn to **17**

162

You cast the STEALTH spell to become a shadow, and then make your move. You know that the spell will not last long, so you set off quickly.

(Roll a six-sided die. If you score a 3 or less, you manage to make it around Cerebus and out through the door. If you score anything else, you waited a little too long and the claws of the beast strike you as you leave. Lose TWO Health Grades).

- If you survive, turn to **17**

163

You cast the AGILITY spell and your body gains an almost inhuman speed, allowing you to run and move quicker than normal. You know the spell will not last long, so you make your move quickly.

(Roll a six-sided die. If you score a 3 or less, you manage to make it around Cerebus and through the door. If you score anything else, you waited a little too long and the claws of the beast strike you as you leave. Lose TWO Health Grades).

- If you survive, turn to **17**

164

You step through the door and unwittingly into a portal. You find yourself in what looks like a study. In front of you, is a table with a stack of papers on it. You read the top of the first page. It reads 'THE LOST ANGEL,' a novel by Adam C. Mitchell.

Then, overhead, you hear a voice. "Oh, hey, Warrior... it's me, Adam! Yes, the author.... It seems that you've stumbled out of your book. Oh well, these things happen. No easy job, but hey, as you've gotten this far in your book, how about a little reward? Go on, have a read. It's a film noir crime caper...."

You move to the first page and begin to read his novel...

'The unforgiving night closed in. Rain had begun to fall, like angry tears of the Almighty. The wet, harsh, cold air stung my face and burnt my lungs. Dim and broken streetlights bathed the maze of seedy back alleys in a ghostly light. The dim light bouncing off upturned garbage cans and the eyes of a stray cat looked towards the commotion. A washed-out drunk took a second to turn away from his bottle, to look on at the chance of spare change, but instead, went back to drowning his sorrows. I stopped to catch my breath. The grim silence was deafened by heavy breathing and my pounding heart. Taxis and trams, passing in the distance, permeated the stillness. Footsteps approached, urging me on; fear pushed my aching legs, despite the pain shooting through them.'

164 Continued

'Turning a corner, I clambered over upturned dustbins and an old, damp fence, scraping my face on a rusty nail. Arriving on a broad street, with little place to hunker down and lie low, I had no choice but to push my legs harder still. They gave way after a hundred yards or so and I tripped, falling to my knees and sliding on the wet cobbles. Pain raced through my left knee, a distant reminder of the crippling cold that had destroyed it during the Siege of Bastogne in '44, and then, the slog of life in post-war limbo afterwards.'

You are about to turn over to another page when Adam stops you. "Well, that's enough.... don't want to give away the plot or anything. Time to go back to your book! Now, hop to it."

(For more information about this novel, please look at the next page)!

- Now, Warrior, turn to **46**

Created using the GameBook Authoring Tool
http://www.crumblyheadgames.co.uk/the-game-book-authoring-tool/

This gamebook features an excerpt from Adam C. Mitchell's crime noir novel, The Lost Angel, and also pays tribute to Dr. Graham Wilson's gamebook, Rise of the Ancients: Bruidd and David Lowrie's gamebook, Shadow Thief, Book 1: Jailbreak.

All three are available for purchase on Amazon and its affiliate markets.